The Sled

and other
Fox & Rabbit Stories

For my neighbor, pal, and fellow juggler,
Paige
—D. McPhail

For Kay and Okie,
my guiding lights.
—J.O'Connor

FIRST FLIGHT® is a registered trademark of Fitzhenry & Whiteside.

Text Copyright © 1999 by David McPhail
Illustration Copyright © 1999 by John O'Connor

First published in the United States in 1999.

Fitzhenry & Whiteside acknowledges with thanks the support of the Government of Canada through its Book Publishing Industry Development Program in the publication of this title.

Printed in Hong Kong.
Cover and book design by Wycliffe Smith Design.

10 9 8 7 6 5 4 3 2 1

Canadian Cataloguing in Publication Data

McPhail, David, 1940
The sled and other fox & rabbit stories
(A first flight level one reader)
"First flight books."

ISBN 1-55041-515-8 (bound)
ISBN 1-55041-517-4 (pbk.)

I. O'Connor, John, 1947-   II. Title.   III. Title: Sled and other fox and
       rabbit stories.   IV. Series: First flight reader

PZ7.M24Sl 1999   jC813'.54   C99-931306-1

A First Flight® Level One Reader

The Sled

and other

Fox & Rabbit Stories

by
David McPhail

Illustrated
by
John O'Connor

Fitzhenry & Whiteside • Toronto

Fox and Rabbit
Story One

Fox ran to Rabbit's house.

Fox ran fast.

Fox ran over.

Fox ran under.

Fox ran right past
Rabbit's house.

Rabbit ran right after Fox.
"Come back!" said Rabbit.

Fox came back.

"I'm glad you saw me,"
said Fox.

"I'm glad, too," said Rabbit.

Peas and Carrots
Story Two

Rabbit asked Fox
to come for supper.

"May we have rabbit
for supper?" said Fox.

"We will have peas and carrots and mashed potatoes," said Rabbit.

"Too bad," said Fox.
"I want rabbit."

Fox came for supper.

"Close your eyes," said Rabbit.
Fox closed his eyes.

"Now open your eyes,"
said Rabbit.
Fox opened his eyes.

Fox saw a big white rabbit.

The rabbit had green eyes
and orange ears.

Fox ate the big white rabbit.

Rabbit ate mashed
potatoes, carrots and peas.

The Sled
Story Three

Fox and Rabbit made a sled.

When they sat on the sled,
it did not move.

"I will push," said Rabbit.
Rabbit pushed, but the sled
went too slow.

"I will push, too," said Fox.
Both Rabbit and Fox pushed
the sled, but it still went
too slow.

Fox and Rabbit were tired from pushing the sled.

They sat down to rest.

The sled started to move.

The sled went fast.

"This is fun!" said Fox.

"Yes," said Rabbit. "This is fun!"

FIRST FLIGHT®

*FIRST FLIGHT® is an exciting
new series of beginning readers.
The series presents titles which include songs,
poems, adventures, mysteries, and humor
by established authors and illustrators.
FIRST FLIGHT® makes the introduction to
reading fun and satisfying
for the young reader.*

*FIRST FLIGHT® is available in 4 levels
to correspond to reading development.*

Level 1 – Preschool - Grade 1
Large type, repetition of simple concepts that are perfect
for reading aloud, easy vocabulary and endearing
characters in short simple stories for the earliest reader.

Level 2 – Grade 1 - Grade 3
Longer sentences, higher level of vocabulary, repetition,
and high-interest stories for the progressing reader.

Level 3 – Grade 2 - Grade 4
Simple stories with more involved plots and a simple
chapter format for the newly independent reader.

Level 4 – Grade 3 - up (First Flight Chapter Books)
More challenging level, minimal illustrations for the
independent reader.

Other Books in the First Flight® Series

Level 1 – Preschool - Grade 1
Fishes in the Ocean *written by* Maggee Spicer *and* Richard Thompson, *and illustrated by* Barbara Hartmann
Then and Now *written by* Richard Thompson, *and illustrated by* Barbara Hartmann
There is Music in a Pussycat *written by* Richard Thompson, *and illustrated by* Barbara Hartmann

Level 2 – Grade 1 - Grade 3
Flying Lessons *written and illustrated by* Celia Godkin
Jingle Bells *written and illustrated by* Maryann Kovalski
Omar On Ice *written and illustrated by* Maryann Kovalski
Rain, Rain *written and illustrated by* Maryann Kovalski
No Frogs for Dinner *written by* Freida Wishinsky, *and illustrated by* Linda Hendry

Level 3 – Grade 2 - Grade 4
Andrew's Magnificent Mountain of Mittens *written by* Deanne Lee Bingham, *and illustrated by* Kim LaFave
Andrew, Catch That Cat! *written by* Deanne Lee Bingham, *and illustrated by* Kim LaFave
Ellen's Terrible TV Troubles *written by* Rachna Gilmore, *and illustrated by* John Mardon

Level 4 – Grade 3 - up (First Flight Chapter Books)
The Money Boot *written by* Ginny Russell, *and illustrated by* John Mardon
Fangs & Me *written by* Rachna Gilmore, *and illustrated by* Gordon Sauvé
More Monsters in School *written by* Martyn Godfrey, *and illustrated by* John Mardon
Emma's Emu *written by* Ken Oppel, *and illustrated by* Kim LaFave